HAWTHORNE
Illustrated

adaptedclassics.com

kristinadesignz.com   artwriteproductions.com

HAWTHORNE *Illustrated*

THREE STORIES BY
NATHANIEL HAWTHORNE

ADAPTED BY:
JEROME TILLER
ILLUSTRATED BY:
MARC JOHNSON-PENCOOK

The *Adapted Classics* Collection

Contemporary-classic illustrations in *Adapted Classics* books add expression to visually-rich stories by world-famous authors. Lightly modified and illustrated to suit and attract modern young readers, stories in the *Adapted Classics* collection are respectful renditions of timeless stories from the world of classic literature.

View the entire collection at: www.adaptedclassics.com

PREFACE

You are about to read adapted versions of three stories by Nathaniel Hawthorne, one of the world's all-time greatest authors. Some changes (paragraph breaks, rearrangements, minor additions and omissions, etc.) were made to accommodate the illustration of characters and critical scenes in the story. Some changes (word choice, word order, etc.) were made to expand its accessibility and appeal, keeping modern youth in mind. No change was made with the notion it would improve the text or the story.

Among other places, the original version of each story can be found at: http://www. gutenberg.org/

CONTENTS

DR. HEIDEGGER'S EXPERIMENT

Old Dr. Heidegger was a very strange man whose unconventional behavior gave rise to a thousand fantastic stories. He was sometimes a little beside himself, as old people often are when worried by present troubles or woeful memories. The same could be said of the four old friends he invited over to his study for an experiment.

Among them was the reclusive Widow Wycherly. She dropped into deep seclusion many years ago when scandalous stories about her circulated in high society, but upon receiving the doctor's invitation, she decided she would emerge from hiding and participate in his experiment.

Doctor Heidegger also invited three gentlemen friends to participate, and all of them agreed. It is worth mentioning that each of these gentlemen, Mr. Medbourne, Colonel Killigrew, and Mr. Gascoigne, were early lovers of the Widow Wycherly. Once they had been on the verge of cutting each other's throats for her sake, but that was many years ago.

All of these gentlemen, and the Widow Wycherly, too, are nothing but melancholy old creatures now. They have led lives filled with misfortune, with their greatest misfortune being that they had not been buried long ago in their graves.

The Widow Wycherly had once been a great beauty, but a life of lonely seclusion rendered her beauty useless until not a speck of it remained. At present she is nothing but a shriveled up old prune.

In his youth Mr. Medbourne had been a prosperous businessman, but he lost all his wealth by frantic speculation. Now everything accounted for, he amounts to not much more than a common beggar.

Colonel Killigrew wasted his best years and his health and wealth chasing sinful pleasures. Now he has nothing to show for his misbehavior but a brood of pains and a nagging conscience.

Mr. Gascoigne was a ruined politician and a man of evil fame. But time has so completely removed him from the knowledge of the present generation that he is now totally obscure — unknown and unnoticed by all.

When all his guests had arrived, Dr. Heidegger motioned everyone to be seated. "My dear old friends," he said. "Welcome to my study. So nice to see all of you again."

Dr. Heidegger's study was a curious place indeed. Cobwebs spanned every corner and antique dust coated almost every surface. Over in the darkest corner of the study stood a tall, narrow, oaken closet with its door cracked open just enough to reveal a skeleton within. Several oaken bookcases lined the walls around the study, and each one was filled with medical texts and notebooks. On the bottom shelf of each of them rested gigantic journals, and standing atop the central bookcase was a bronze bust of Hippocrates, the ancient father of modern medicine; it has been said that Dr. Heidegger consulted face to face with this bust regarding all the difficult cases of his medical practice.

Between two of the bookcases hung a high and dusty mirror set within a tarnished gold frame. It was fabled the spirits of all the doctor's deceased patients dwelt within this mirror and stared at him whenever he turned to face it.

Ornamenting the wall on the side of the study opposite this mirror was a faded, full-length portrait of a young lady dressed in silk, satin, and brocade. Over half a century ago Dr. Heidegger had been on the point of marrying this young lady until, on the eve of their wedding, feeling a bit under the weather, she swallowed one of his prescriptions and died on the spot.

"My dear old friends," repeated Dr. Heidegger, "in my invitation I asked you to assist me in one of the little experiments that I conduct here in my study to amuse myself. Now, before proceeding further, I ask you once again. Can I count on your help in performing an exceedingly curious experiment?"

Without waiting for a reply, Dr. Heidegger hobbled across the chamber.

The doctor's four guests anticipated nothing more curious than the murder of a mouse in an air pump or the examination of a cobweb by the microscope, or some similar nonsensical experiment that the doctor had been known to conduct in his study. But Dr. Heidegger returned with the huge book that was bound in black leather, the one commonly reported to be a book of magic.

Undoing the silver clasps, he opened the volume and took from among its pages a rose, or what was once a rose. For now the green leaves and crimson petals had assumed a brownish hue, and the ancient flower seemed ready to crumble to dust in the doctor's hands.

"This withered and crumbling rose," said Dr. Heidegger, with a sigh, "blossomed five and fifty years ago. Sylvia Ward, whose portrait hangs there, gave it to me, and I meant to wear it in my lapel at our wedding. For fifty-five years I have kept it pressed between the leaves of this old volume. Now, would any one of you think that this old, withered rose could ever bloom again?"

"Nonsense!" said the Widow Wycherly, with a peevish toss of her head. "You might as well ask whether an old woman's wrinkled face could ever bloom again."

"Look!" answered Dr. Heidegger.

He uncovered the vase and threw the faded rose into the water. At first it lay lightly on the surface of the fluid, appearing to absorb none of its moisture. Soon, however, an amazing change began to take place. The crushed and dried petals stirred and assumed a deepening tinge of crimson and the slender stalk and twigs of foliage became green.

And just like that, the half-century-old rose was looking as fresh as when Sylvia Ward had first given it to her lover.

"That is certainly a very clever deception. How did you do it?" remarked Mr. Gascoigne, offhandedly. He had seen greater miracles at a magician's show.

"Did you never hear of the 'Fountain of Youth'?" asked Dr. Heidegger, "which Ponce De Leon, the Spanish adventurer, went in search of two or three centuries ago?"

"Yes, I have. But did Ponce De Leon ever find it?" asked the Widow Wycherly.

"No," answered Dr. Heidegger, "he never looked in the right place. According to an acquaintance of mine, the famous Fountain of Youth is situated in the southern part of Florida, not far from Lake Macaco. He tells me that several gigantic magnolia trees overshadow the source of the fountain and, even though they are countless centuries old, this wonderful water has kept them as fresh as daisies. My acquaintance, knowing my curiosity about such things, sent me what you see in the vase."

"Ahem!" said Colonel Killigrew, who didn't believe a word of the doctor's story; "and what may be the effect of this fluid on humans?"

"You shall judge for yourself, my dear colonel," replied Dr. Heidegger; "and all of you, my respected friends, are welcome to as much of this admirable fluid as may restore to you the bloom of youth. As for me, having had much trouble in growing old, I am in no hurry to grow young again. Therefore, with your permission, I will merely watch the progress of the experiment."

While he spoke, Dr. Heidegger filled the four champagne glasses with the water of the Fountain of Youth. Little bubbles rose from the depths of the glasses of water and burst in silvery spray at the surface, diffusing a pleasant perfume.

The old people didn't doubt that the water possessed pleasant and flavorful properties; and although utterly skeptical as to its restorative power, they were inclined to swallow it at once.

But Dr. Heidegger asked them to wait a moment.

"Before you drink, my respectable old friends," said he, "I suggest that you reflect upon your lifetime experiences and jot down a few general rules that will guide you in passing through the perils of youth a second time. You have lived through youth once. Think what a sin and shame it would be if you did not use that peculiar advantage to become examples of virtue and wisdom to all the young people of the present age!"

The doctor's four friends made no response, except by their feeble and tremulous laughter. They all knew how closely repentance treads behind the steps of error, so it was ridiculous for them to suppose that they could ever go astray again.

"Drink, then," said the doctor, bowing: "I'm overjoyed that I did such a good job selecting the subjects of my experiment."

With palsied hands, the doctor's four old friends raised the glasses to their lips. The water, if it really did possess the virtues Dr. Heidegger claimed, could not have been gifted to four people who needed it more.

They looked as if they had never known what youth or pleasure was. They looked as if they had always been the gray, decrepit, miserable creatures who now stooped round the doctor's table—sapless creatures without life enough in their souls or bodies to be animated even by the prospect of growing young again.

They drank the water and replaced their glasses on the table. Almost immediately there was an improvement in the tone of the party, not unlike what might have been produced by a generous glass of wine. At once a sudden glow of cheerful sunshine brightened over all their faces.

A healthful ruddiness was on their cheeks instead of the ashen hue that had made them look so corpse-like.

They gazed at one another, and fancied that some magic power had really begun to smooth away the deep and sad inscriptions that Father Time had been so long engraving on their brows.

The Widow Wycherly adjusted her widows bun, for she felt almost like a woman again.

"Give us more of this wondrous water!" they cried eagerly. "We are younger—but we are still too old! Quick—give us more to drink!"

"Patience, patience!" said Dr. Heidegger, who sat watching the experiment with philosophic coolness. "You have been a long time growing old. What—you need now to grow young again in half an hour? Ah, but don't let me stand in your way. The water is at your service."

Again he filled their glasses with the liquor of youth, enough of which still remained in the vase to turn half the old people in the city to the age of their own grandchildren.

While bubbles yet sparkled on the brims of the glasses, the doctor's four guests snatched the glasses from the table and swallowed the contents at a single gulp.

Was it delusion? Even while the fluid was passing down their throats, it seemed to be causing their whole systems to change. Their eyes grew clear and bright. A dark shade deepened their silvery hairs. And there they sat around the table, three gentlemen of middle age, and a woman hardly beyond her curvaceous prime.

"My dear widow, you are charming!" cried Colonel Killigrew, whose eyes had been fixed upon her face while the shadows of age were flitting from it like darkness from the crimson daybreak.

The fair widow knew from past experience that Colonel Killigrew's compliments were not always measured by sober truth, so she started up and ran to the mirror, still dreading that she would see the ugly reflection of an old woman there.

Meanwhile, the three gentlemen behaved as if the water of the Fountain of Youth possessed some intoxicating qualities, unless, instead, their bursting spirits were caused by the sudden removal of the weight of years.

Mr. Medbourne made a calculation of the money he could make supplying the East Indies with ice by harnessing a team of whales to the polar icecaps.

Colonel Killigrew sang a jolly bottle song and ringed his glass in symphony while his eyes wandered toward the buxom figure of the Widow Wycherly.

Mr. Gascoigne's mind ran on political topics, but it couldn't easily be discerned whether he was referring to the past, present, or future. He rattled out full-throated sentences about patriotism, national glory, and people's rights, just as politicians from every era do.

As for the Widow Wycherly, she stood before the mirror primping, curtseying, simpering and greeting her own image as the friend whom she loved better than all the world beside.

She thrust her face close to the glass to see whether some long-remembered wrinkle or crow's foot had indeed vanished. She examined whether the snow had really melted from her hair and wondered how to refashion the outdated widow's bun atop her head.

At last, turning briskly away, she came with a sort of dancing step to the table.

"My dear old doctor," cried she, "pray favor me with another glass!"

"Certainly, my dear madam, certainly!" replied the agreeable doctor. "See! I have already filled the glasses."

There stood the four glasses full to the brim with this wonderful water. From the surface of the water sparkled a delicate spray resembling the glitter of diamonds.

It was now so near sunset that the study had grown duskier than ever, but a mild and moon-like splendor gleamed from within the vase and rested on the four guests and Doctor Heidegger. The eyes of the four guests were on the doctor while they gulped the third glass of the Fountain of Youth.

There he sat in a high back, elaborately carved, oaken armchair, with an aura of gray dignity, and they were almost awed by the expression on his mysterious face. His look would have befitted Father Time, whose power had never before been disputed.

Never disputed, never before, save now by these fortunate guests, for in a flash the exhilarating gush of young life shot through their veins. The doctor's guests were now in the happy prime of youth. Age, with its miserable train of cares and sorrows and diseases, was remembered only as the trouble of a dream from which they had joyously awoke. The fresh gloss of the soul, so early lost, again threw its enchantment over all their prospects. They felt like new-created beings in a new-created universe.

"We are young! We are young!" they cried exultingly.

Just as old age had rubbed out the strongly marked characteristics of middle life, so now youth did the same. The doctor's guests were a group of merry youngsters now, almost maddened with the frolicky exuberance of their youth. The most singular effect of their gaiety was an impulse to mock the infirmity and decrepitude of old age. They laughed loudly at their old-fashioned attire, the wide-skirted coats and flapped waistcoats of the young men, and the ancient gown of the blooming girl. One of them limped across the floor like a gouty grandfather. One set a pair of spectacles astride of his nose and pretended to pore over the black-letter pages of the book of magic. A third seated himself in an armchair and tried to imitate the venerable dignity of Dr. Heidegger. Then they all shouted mirthfully and leaped about the room. The Widow Wycherly—if so fresh a damsel could be called a widow—tripped up to the doctor's chair with mischievous merriment in her rosy face. "Doctor, you dear old soul," cried she, "get up out of that chair and dance with me!"

And then the four young people laughed louder than ever, to think what a queer figure the poor old doctor would cut.

"Please excuse me," answered the doctor quietly. "I am old and rheumatic, and my dancing days were over long ago. But either of these merry young gentlemen will be glad to take so pretty a partner as you."

"Dance with me, Clara!" cried Colonel Killigrew

"No, no, I will be her partner!" shouted Mr. Gascoigne.

"She promised me her hand fifty years ago!" exclaimed Mr. Medbourne.

They all gathered round her. One passionately grasped both her hands in his. Another threw his arm about her waist. The third buried his hand among the glossy curls that clustered beside her redone bun. Blushing, panting, struggling, chiding, laughing, her warm breath fanning each of their faces by turns, the girl-widow strove to disengage herself, yet still remained in their triple embrace.

Never was there a livelier picture of youth rivaling for the prize of bewitching beauty. Yet, by a strange deception, owing to the duskiness of the study and the antique dresses they still wore, the tall mirror is said to have reflected the figures of three gray, withered, old geezers ridiculously contending for the skinny ugliness of a shriveled old hag.

But they were young: their burning passions proved them so. Inflamed to madness by the flirting of the girl-widow, who neither granted nor quite withheld her favors, the three rivals began to interchange threatening glances. Still keeping hold of the fair prize, they grappled fiercely at one another's throats. As they struggled to and fro, the table was overturned, and the vase dashed into a thousand fragments.

The precious Water of Youth flowed in a bright stream across the floor, moistening the wings of a butterfly, which, grown old in the decline of summer, had alighted there to die. Rejuvenated by the water, the insect took flight, fluttered lightly through the study, and settled on the mealy scalp of Dr. Heidegger.

"Come, come, gentlemen! Come, Madam Wycherly,"
exclaimed the doctor, "I really must protest against
this riot."

They stood still and shivered, for it seemed as if gray Time
were calling them back from their sunny youth, far down
into the chill and dark vale of years. They looked at old Dr.
Heidegger, who sat in his carved armchair holding the rose
of half a century ago, which he had rescued from among
the fragments of the shattered vase.

At the motion of his hand, the four rioters resumed their
seats, and readily so, for their violent exertions had
wearied them, youthful though they were.

"My poor Sylvia's rose!" cried Dr. Heidegger, holding it to
show in the light of the sunset clouds. "It appears to be
fading again."

And so it was. Even while the party was looking at it,
the flower continued to shrivel, more and more, until it
became as dry and fragile as when the doctor had first
thrown it into the vase. He shook off the few drops of
moisture that clung to its petals.

"I love it as well like this as in its dewy freshness," observed he, pressing the withered rose to his withered lips. While he spoke, the butterfly fluttered down from atop the doctor's head and fell upon the floor.

His guests shivered again. A strange chilliness, whether of the body or spirit they could not tell, was creeping gradually over them all.

They gazed at one another and fancied that each fleeting moment snatched away a charm and left a deepening furrow where none had been before.

Was it an illusion? Had the changes of a lifetime been crowded into so brief a space, and were they now four aged people, sitting with their old friend, Dr. Heidegger?

"Are we grown old again, so soon?" they cried.

In truth they had. The Water of Youth possessed merely a virtue more passing than that of wine. The delirium it created had effervesced away. Yes! They were old again.

With a shuddering impulse that showed her a woman still, the widow clasped her skinny hands before her face and wished that the coffin lid were over it, since it could no longer be beautiful.

"Yes, friends, you are old again," said Dr. Heidegger, "and lo and behold! The Water of Youth is all lavished on the ground. Well—I don't bemoan it; for even if the fountain gushed at my very doorstep, I would not stoop to bathe my lips in it—no, even if its delirium were for years instead of moments. Such is the lesson you have taught me!"

But the doctor's four friends had taught no such lesson to themselves. They resolved forthwith to make a pilgrimage to Florida, and drink at morning, noon, and night from the Fountain of Youth.

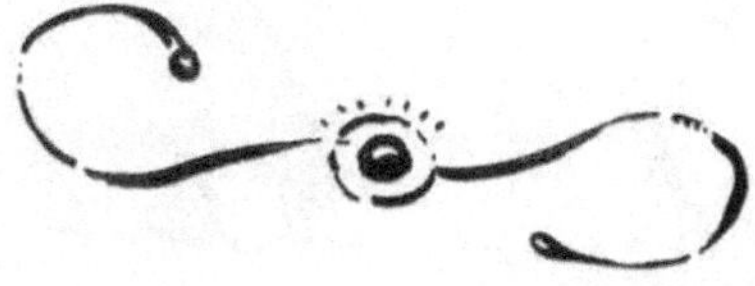

the end

DR. HEIDEGGER'S EXPERIMENT

The long-defunct Knickerbocker magazine first published this story under the title "The Fountain of Youth" in 1837. Lewis G. Clark, editor of the magazine, commented to Hawthorne "I have rarely read anything which delighted me more". Later, the famous American author and literary critic Edgar Allan Poe described "Dr. Heidegger's Experiment" as "exceedingly well-imagined and executed with surpassing ability".

Hawthorne was nearly obsessed with the idea of eternal youth, a theme he incorporated into other stories as well. Since he was an astute critic of society who possessed a remarkable imagination, it's fun to wonder whether Hawthorne could have foreseen future industries built upon the foundational desire to never leave youth behind.

"Dr. Heidegger's Experiment" is a moral allegory, which is a story that uses symbolism to make a moral point. Hawthorne commonly used this technique in his fiction. It also contains gothic elements—settings, objects, and characters that are otherworldly. As with allegories, Hawthorne often used gothic elements in his fiction.

Describing his writing workroom, Hawthorne said: "This deserves to be called a haunted chamber, for thousands and thousands of visions have appeared to me in it." Many of those visions must have went into the making of this marvelous, highly visual story.

MR. HIGGINBOTHAM'S CATASTROPHE

Dominicus Pike was a young man of excellent character. He drove a smart little mare that pulled a neat little cart from which he peddled saleable goods. He sold licorice sticks and lollipops, ointments and elixirs, pots and pans, and more goods to merchants and folks in towns and villages throughout New England. Dominicus was keen at a bargain, a trait that sits well with New England Yankees who, as it has been said, would rather be shaved with a sharp razor than a dull one.

He was also especially beloved by the pretty girls throughout Connecticut whose favor he courted with presents of the choicest candies in his stock. But most notably, Dominicus was inquisitive and something of a tattler. He was ever-itching to hear the news and always anxious to tell it again.

One day after an early breakfast at Morristown, Dominicus set out for the village of Parker's Falls on the Salmon River. By seven o'clock he was uncomfortably eager to hold a morning gossip; he had traveled seven miles through a solitary piece of woods without speaking a word to anybody but himself and his little gray mare.

An opportunity for gossip seemed at hand when Dominicus saw a man coming over the brow of the hill at the foot of which he had stopped his cart. The man toted a bundle that hung over his shoulder at the end of a stick. He descended the hill traveling at a weary, yet determined pace; he looked as if he had two-footed it all night and meant to do the same all day.

"Good morning, mister," said Dominicus, when within speaking distance.

"I see you've gone a pretty good jog," remarked Dominicus. "What's the latest news at Parker's Falls?"

The man pulled the broad brim of a gray hat over his eyes. He looked like the kind of fellow you wouldn't want to meet in a solitary woods. "I did not come from Parker's Falls," he said.

 "Well, then," said Dominicus Pike, "let's have the latest news from where you did come. I'm not particular about Parker's Falls. Any place will do."

Prodded thus for information, the traveler appeared to hesitate a little, either as if he was searching his memory for news or weighing whether or not he should tell it. Then he mounted the step of the little cart and whispered in the ear of Dominicus, though he could have shouted and no other human would have heard him.

"I do remember one little trifle of news," said he. "Old Mr. Higginbotham of Kimballton was murdered in his orchard at eight o'clock last night by an Irishman and an Ethiopian. They strung him up to the branch of a St. Michael's pear tree where nobody would find him till the morning."

As soon as this horrible information was communicated, the traveler lit out and resumed his journey with more speed than ever. Dominicus called out, offered him a lollipop, and invited him to relate all the particulars of the story, but the traveler did not look back.

Dominicus knew Mr. Higginbotham; he had paid regular visits to his store and sold him many bunches of licorice sticks and a great deal of ointment and elixir. He pondered on the old man's fate and was rather astonished at how fast the news about his murder had spread. Kimballton was nearly sixty miles distant in a straight line; the murder had been committed at eight o'clock the preceding night, yet Dominicus heard of it at seven in the morning. Why, in all probability, poor Mr. Higginbotham's own family would have just now discovered his corpse hanging on the St. Michael's pear tree. The traveler on foot must have worn winged boots to travel at such a high rate of speed.

"Man o' man," thought Dominicus Pike. "Ill-news travels fast, but this beats railroads. That fellow ought to be hired to go express with the President's message."

Dominicus was perplexed by this space and time puzzle, but he settled the difficulty by supposing the stranger had made a one-day mistake in the date of the murder. By arriving at this conclusion, Dominicus freed himself to tell the story, and he did, many times.

That day he introduced the story to at least twenty horrified audiences at inns and country-stores along the road. Invariably, he found himself to be the first bearer of the news each time he told it, and he was so pestered with questions at every telling that he could not avoid filling up the outline until it became quite a respectable story, flush with details.

During one telling of it, he met with a piece of corroborating evidence. A clerk that used to work at Mr. Higginbotham's store testified that the old gentleman was accustomed to return home through the orchard about nightfall with the money and valuable papers of his store in his pocket. The clerk showed but little grief at Mr. Higginbotham's catastrophe. He hinted what the peddler had discovered in his own dealings at the store—that Mr. Higginbotham was a crusty old fellow as tight as a vise. The clerk also mentioned that the Higginbotham property would descend to a pretty niece who was now keeping school in Kimballton.

What with telling the news for the public good and driving bargains for his own good, Dominicus was so much delayed on the road that he chose to put himself up at an inn about five miles short of Parker's Falls. After supper, with one of his prime lollipops wedged between his cheek and gum, he seated himself in the parlor and once again went through the story of the murder, which had grown so big, so fast, that it took him half an hour to tell it.

There were as many as twenty people in the room at the time, nineteen of whom took it for gospel. But the twentieth person was an elderly farmer who had arrived on horseback a short time before. He was now seated in a corner, smoking his pipe. When the story was concluded, he rose up very deliberately, brought his chair right in front of Dominicus, stared him full in the face, and puffed out the vilest tobacco-smoke the peddler had ever smelt.

"Will you make an affidavit," demanded he, in the tone of a country-justice examining a witness, "that old Squire Higginbotham of Kimballton was murdered in his orchard the night before last and found hanging on his great pear tree yesterday morning?"

"I tell the story as I heard it, mister," answered Dominicus, dropping his half-finished lolly. "I don't say that I saw the thing done, so I can't take my oath that he was murdered exactly in that way."

"But I can take mine," said the farmer, "that if Squire Higginbotham was murdered the night before last, I drank a glass of bitters with his ghost this morning. Being a neighbor of mine, he called me into his store as I was riding by, and treated me, and then asked me to do a little business for him on the road. He didn't seem to know any more about his own murder than I did."

"Why, then it can't be a fact!" exclaimed Dominicus Pike.

"I guess he'd have mentioned it if it was," said the old farmer; and he removed his chair back to the corner, leaving Dominicus quite down in the mouth.

Now here was a sad resurrection of old Mr. Higginbotham! The peddler had no heart to mingle in the conversation any more, so he went to bed, where all night long he dreamed of hanging on the St. Michael's pear tree.

To avoid the old farmer (whom he detested so much that suspending him from a tree would have pleased him better than proof of Mr. Higginbotham's hanging), Dominicus rose in the gray of the morning, hooked the little mare into the little cart and trotted swiftly away toward Parker's Falls.

The fresh breeze, the dewy road, and the pleasant summer dawn revived his spirits, and might have encouraged him to repeat the old story had there been anybody awake to hear it. But he met neither ox-team, light wagon, carriage, horseman nor foot-traveler until, just as he crossed Salmon River, a man came trudging down to the bridge with a bundle on the end of a stick balanced over his shoulder.

"Good-morning, mister," said the peddler, reining in his mare. "If you come from Kimballton or that neighborhood, maybe you can tell me the real fact about this affair of old Mr. Higginbotham. Was the old fellow actually murdered two or three nights ago by an Irishman and an Ethiopian?"

Dominicus had spoken in too great a hurry to see at first that the stranger himself had a deep tinge of African blood. On hearing this sudden question, the stranger appeared to change his skin, its golden hue becoming more like a ghastly white.

While shaking and stammering, he thus replied: "No, no! There was no man of color. It was an Irishman that hanged him last night at eight o'clock; I came away at seven. His folks can't have looked for him in the orchard yet."

Scarcely had the man spoken these words when he interrupted himself and, though he seemed weary enough before, continued his journey at a pace that would have kept the peddler's mare on a smart trot.

Dominicus stared after him in great perplexity. If the murder had not been committed till Tuesday night, who was that prophet that had foretold the murder in all its circumstances on Tuesday morning? And if Mr. Higginbotham's corpse were not yet discovered by his own family, how did this man on this road some thirty miles distant from Kimballton know that he was hanging in the orchard, especially since this man had left there before the unfortunate Mr. Higginbotham was hanged at all?

These ambiguous circumstances, coupled with the stranger's surprise and terror, made Dominicus think of raising a hue-and-cry after him as an accomplice in the murder, since a murder, it seemed, really had been committed. "But let the poor devil go," said the peddler to himself. "I don't want his blood on my head, and capturing him wouldn't unhang Mr. Higginbotham."

Then Dominicus pondered on what he had just heard himself say. "Unhang the old gentleman? It's a sin, I know, but I should hate to have him come back to life a second time and make me a liar."

With these thoughts, Dominicus Pike drove into the street of Parker's Falls, which was as thriving a village as three cotton-factories and a mill could make it. The cotton machinery was not in motion and only a few of the store shop doors were unlocked when he alighted in the stable-yard of the inn.

He made it his first business to order his mare four quarts of oats. His second duty, of course, was to reveal Mr. Higginbotham's catastrophe to the hostler who tended his mare, and then to every man, woman, and child he could find to tell the story.

He decided, however, not to be too positive as to the date of the direful act, and he also made sure to be uncertain whether it was committed by an Irishman and an Ethiopian or by an Irishman alone. Neither did he claim to relate it on his own authority or that of any one person, but mentioned it as a report that was generally known.

The story ran through the town like fire among dead trees and became so much the talk about town that nobody could tell from whom it had originated. Mr. Higginbotham was as well known at Parker's Falls as any citizen of the place, being part-owner of the mill and a considerable stockholder in the cotton factories. The inhabitants felt that their own prosperity was linked with his fate.

There was so much excitement that the Parker's Falls Weekly Gazette was hurriedly printed ahead of its regular day of publication, half of it blank paper and half a column emphasized with capitals and headed "HORRID MURDER OF MR. HIGGINBOTHAM!"

Among other dreadful details, the printed account described the mark of the cord that rounded the dead man's neck and stated the number of thousand of dollars of which he had been robbed. There was much pitiful concern, also, about the distress of his niece, who had gone from one fainting-fit to another ever since her uncle was found hanging on the St. Michael's pear tree with his pockets inside out. The village poet likewise commemorated the young lady's grief in seventeen stanzas of a ballad.

The councilmen held a meeting and, in consideration of Mr. Higginbotham's claims on the town, determined to issue handbills offering a reward of five hundred dollars for the apprehension of his murderers and the recovery of the stolen property.

Meanwhile, the whole population of Parker's Falls, consisting of shopkeepers, mistresses of boarding-houses, factory-girls, mill-men and schoolboys, rushed into the street and kept up such a terrible chatter that it more than compensated for the silence of the cotton-machines, which had refrained from their usual din out of respect to the deceased. Had Mr. Higginbotham cared about fame after death, his untimely ghost would have rejoiced in this noisy commotion.

Our friend Dominicus, in his vanity of heart, forgot his intended precautions and, mounting on the town-pump, announced himself as the bearer of the authentic intelligence which had caused so wonderful a sensation.

He immediately became the great man of the moment, and had just begun a new edition of the narrative with a voice like a field-preacher when the mail-stage drove into the village street. It had traveled all night, and must have shifted horses at Kimballton at three in the morning.

"Now we shall hear all the particulars!" shouted the crowd.

The coach rumbled up to the covered porch of the inn followed by a thousand people; for if there were any who had been minding their own business till then, they now left it to hear the news. The peddler, foremost in the race, discovered two passengers, both of whom had been startled

from a comfortable nap to find themselves in the center of a mob. Every person peppered them with a separate question, all questions asked at once. The couple were struck speechless, even though one was a lawyer. The other member of the twosome was a young lady.

"Mr. Higginbotham! Mr. Higginbotham! Tell us the particulars about old Mr. Higginbotham!" bawled the mob. "What is the coroner's verdict? Are the murderers apprehended? Is Mr. Higginbotham's niece come out of her fainting-fits? Mr. Higginbotham! Mr. Higginbotham!"

The coachman said not a word except to swear awfully at the hostler for not bringing him a fresh team of horses. The lawyer inside had generally his wits about him even when asleep; the first thing he did after learning the cause of the excitement was to produce a large red pocketbook. Meantime, Dominicus Pike, being an extremely polite young man, and also suspecting that a female tongue would tell the story as glibly as a lawyer's, had handed the lady out of the coach. She was a fine, smart girl, now wide awake and bright as a button. She had such a sweet, pretty mouth that Dominicus almost would rather have heard a love-tale from it as a tale of murder.

"Gentlemen and ladies," said the lawyer to the shopkeepers, the mill-men and the factory-girls, "I can assure you that some unaccountable mistake—or, more probably, a willful falsehood maliciously contrived to injure Mr. Higginbotham's credit—has excited this uproar. We passed through Kimballton at three o'clock this morning, and most certainly should have been informed of the murder had any been committed. But I have proof nearly as strong as Mr. Higginbotham's own oral testimony in the negative. Here is a note relating to a suit of his in the Connecticut courts that was delivered to me from that gentleman himself. I find it dated at ten o'clock last evening."

So saying, the lawyer exhibited the date and signature of the note. It irrefutably proved either that this perverse Mr. Higginbotham was alive when he wrote it, or, as some deemed the more probable case of two doubtful ones, that he was so absorbed in worldly business as to continue to transact it even after his death.

But more unexpected evidence was forthcoming. The young lady, after disembarking from the stagecoach, appeared at the tavern door. Merely seizing a moment to smooth her gown and put her curls in order, she made a modest signal to be heard.

"Good people," said she, "I am Mr. Higginbotham's niece."

A wondering murmur passed through the crowd on beholding her so rosy and so bright—that same unhappy niece whom they had supposed, on the authority of the Parker's Falls Weekly Gazette, to be lying at death's door in a fainting-fit (though some shrewd fellows had doubted all along whether a young lady would be quite so desperate at the hanging of a rich old uncle).

"You see," continued Miss Higginbotham, with a smile, "that this strange story is quite unfounded as to myself, and I believe I may affirm it to be equally so in regard to my dear Uncle Higginbotham."

The crowd inched closer to Miss Higginbotham, irresistibly drawn by her beauty and the sweet timbre of her voice. Dominicus Pike, arms outstretched, did as much as he could to block the crowd's advance and maintain his place nearest to the enchanting speaker.

"My uncle has the kindness to give me a home in his house, though I contribute to my own support by teaching a school. I left Kimballton this morning to spend the vacation of commencement-week with a friend about five miles from Parker's Falls. My generous uncle, when he heard me on the stairs, called me to his bedside and gave me two dollars and fifty cents to pay my stage-fare, and another dollar for my extra expenses. He then laid his pocketbook under his pillow, shook hands with me, and advised me to take some biscuit in my bag instead of breakfasting on the road. I feel confident, therefore, that I left my beloved relative alive, and I trust that I shall find him so on my return."

The young lady curtsied at the close of her speech, which was so sensible and well worded, and delivered with such grace and propriety, that everybody thought her fit to be the principal of the best academy in the state. At the same time, the wrath of the inhabitants of Parker's Falls was so excessive on learning of the unfounded information, that a stranger would have supposed Mr. Higginbotham was an object of hate in the town and that its citizens had been thankful for his murder.

Deeply enraged, the townspeople immediately resolved to bestow public honors on the teller of the malicious lie. They only hesitated trying to decide whether to tar and feather Dominicus Pike, ride him on a rail, or refresh him with an unremitting stream of water at the town-pump, the very pump on top of which he had declared himself the bearer of the news.

Meanwhile, the councilmen of Parkers Falls, by advice of the lawyer who had arrived on the stagecoach, considered prosecuting Dominicus for circulating unfounded reports to the great disturbance of the peace of the commonwealth.

Nothing but an eloquent appeal made by the young lady on his behalf saved Dominicus Pike from either mob-law or a court of justice. So freed from punishment because of her, Dominicus addressed a few words of heartfelt gratitude to her, then mounted his little cart and rode out of town under a discharge of artillery from schoolboys, who found plenty of ammunition in the neighboring clay-pits and mud-holes.

As Dominicus turned his head to exchange a farewell glance with Mr. Higginbotham's niece, a mud ball having the consistency of hasty pudding hit him slap in the mouth, giving him a most grim aspect. His whole person was so bespattered with other filthy missiles of this kind that he almost had a mind to ride back and ask for the threatened wash-down at the town-pump; for such water treatment, though not meant to be kind, would have been a deed of charity now. However, the sun shone bright on poor Dominicus as he rode away from town, and the mud—as if an emblem of all stains of undeserved disgrace—was easily brushed off when dry.

Dominicus, being a funny rogue, soon cheered up and gave a hearty laugh at the uproar that his story had excited. Might not the reward-notices the councilmen had printed cause all the vagabonds in the state to be apprehended?

And since the paragraph in the Parker's Falls Weekly Gazette would soon be reprinted all the way from Maine to Florida, and perhaps would be an item in the London newspapers as well, would not many a miser tremble for his moneybags and his life on learning about the catastrophe of Mr. Higginbotham?

As he traveled along, the peddler also meditated with much fervor on the charms of the young schoolmistress. He swore that no one ever spoke or looked so like an angel as Miss Higginbotham while she defended him from the wrathful people at Parker's Falls.

Dominicus was now on the Kimballton turnpike, having all along determined to visit that place to ply his trade. As he approached the scene of the supposed murder, he continually revolved the circumstances of the murder in his mind and was astonished at the aspect the whole case assumed.

Had the second stranger not corroborated the story of the first stranger, Dominicus might now have considered the story a hoax. But the second stranger was evidently acquainted either with the report of the murder or the fact of it. Plus, there was also the dismayed and guilty look on the second stranger's face when Dominicus abruptly questioned him about Mr. Higginbotham's catastrophe.

Add to this singular combination of incidents the rumor which tallied exactly with Mr. Higginbotham's character and habits of life, the fact that Mr. Higginbotham had an orchard and a St. Michael's pear tree near which he always passed at nightfall, plus the circumstantial evidence that appeared so strong, and Dominicus doubted whether the dated signature of Mr. Higginbotham that the lawyer produced or even the niece's direct testimony ought to be thought equivalent to it.

Making cautious inquiries along the road, the peddler further learned that there was an Irishman of doubtful character who worked for Mr. Higginbotham. Content to purchase labor on the cheap, Mr. Higginbotham had hired the man without a recommendation.

Upon reaching the top of a lonely hill, Dominicus Pike exclaimed aloud, "May I be hanged myself if I'll believe that old Higginbotham is unhanged until I see him with my own eyes and hear it from his own mouth. And, as he's a real shaver of the truth, I'll have the minister or some other responsible man witness and endorse the statement."

It was growing dusk when Dominicus approached the toll-house on Kimballton turnpike, about a quarter of a mile from the village of this name. His little mare was fast catching him up to a man on horseback. The man trotted his horse through the gate about thirty yards ahead, nodded to the toll-gatherer and kept on towards the village. Then Dominicus reached the gate. He was acquainted with the toll-man, and while making change the usual remarks on the weather passed between them.

"I suppose," said the peddler, throwing back his whiplash to bring it down like a feather on the mare's flank, "you have not seen anything of old Mr. Higginbotham within a day or two?"

"Yes," answered the toll-gatherer; "he passed the gate just before you drove up. Yonder he rides now, if you can see him through the dusk. He's been to Woodfield this afternoon attending a sheriff's sale. The old man generally shakes hands and has a little chat with me, but tonight he nodded as if to say, 'Charge my toll,' and jogged on. Wherever he goes, he must always be at home by eight o'clock."

"So they tell me," said Dominicus.

"I never saw a man look so yellow and thin as the squire does," continued the toll-gatherer. "I says to myself tonight, 'He's more like a ghost or an old mummy than good flesh and blood.'"

The peddler strained his eyes through the twilight, and could just discern the horseman now far ahead on the village road.

He seemed to recognize the rear of Mr. Higginbotham, but through the evening shadows and amid the dust from the horse's feet, the figure appeared dim and unsubstantial, as if the shape of the mysterious old man were faintly molded of darkness and gray light. Dominicus shivered.

"Mr. Higginbotham has come back from the other world by way of the Kimballton turnpike," thought Dominicus.

He shook the reins and rode forward, keeping about the same distance in the rear of the gray old shadow until it was concealed by a bend of the road.

On reaching this point the peddler no longer saw the man on horseback, but found himself at the head of the village street, not far from a number of stores and two taverns clustered round the meeting-house steeple.

On his left was a stone wall with a gate. It was the boundary of a wood-lot, beyond which lay an orchard. Farther still was a mowing-field, and last of all, a house. Dominicus knew these were the property of Mr. Higginbotham. His little mare stopped short—probably by instinct—for he was not conscious of tightening the reins. Dominicus trembled.

"For the soul of me, I cannot go by this gate!" said he. "I shall never be my own man again till I see whether Mr. Higginbotham is hanging on the St. Michael's pear tree."

He leaped from the cart, spun the rein a turn around the gate-post, and ran along the green path of the wood-lot as if Lucifer were chasing behind him.

Just then the village clock tolled eight, and as each deep stroke sounded, Dominicus made a fresh bound and flew faster than before until, dim in the solitary center of the orchard, he saw the fated pear tree.

One great branch stretched from the old contorted trunk across the path and threw the darkest shadow on that one spot of the path. But something seemed to struggle beneath the branch!

The peddler had never pretended to be more courageous than befits a peaceable man, nor could he account for his valor on this awful emergency. Certain it is, however, that he rushed forward, downed a sturdy Irishman with the butt-end of his whip, and found—not hanging on the St. Michael's pear tree, but trembling beneath it with a halter round his neck—the old identical Mr. Higginbotham.

"Mr. Higginbotham," said Dominicus, tremulously, "you're an honest man, and I'll take your word for it. Have you been hanged, or not?"

As soon as he was satisfied that Mr. Higginbotham had not been hanged, Dominicus set about discovering the simple explanation of how a coming event was made to cast its shadow before.

It turned out that three men had actually plotted the robbery and murder of Mr. Higginbotham. Successively, two of them lost courage and fled. The traveler that Dominicus met in the solitary woods was the first conspirator to lose his courage and flee. He left Kimbaltown in the afternoon before the evening of the planned murder. Upon discovering they had been deserted, the remaining two conspirators made new plans and postponed the crime by one night. But then the Ethiopian lost courage and fled, and so the Irishman postponed the crime one more night, and it was he who was in the act of committing the crime when a champion, blindly obeying the call of fate like the heroes of old, appeared. That champion, of course, was the peddler, Dominicus Pike.

From that time forward, Mr. Higginbotham took the peddler into high favor, sanctioned his courtship of the pretty schoolmistress and settled his whole property on their children, allowing the parents the interest. In due time the old gentleman capped the climax of his favors by dying a Christian death in bed. Since that melancholy event, Dominicus Pike moved from Kimballton and established a large candy factory in Parkers Falls and, letting bygones be bygones, employed men who, when boys, had once bespattered him with mud.

the end

MR. HIGGINBOTHAM'S CATASTROPHE

Nathaniel Hawthorne's earliest collection of stories and sketches was titled "Twice Told Tales". In addition to "Dr. Heidegger's Experiment" and many other gothic tales, the collection included "Mr. Higginbotham's Catastrophe", a story that Hawthorne told in a light, humorous vein. Besides departing from his normal, eerie style, it differed from most of his work because it carries no great moral message.

Unusual though it is, Edgar Alan Poe, a contemporary of Hawthorne and a renowned literary critic, praised "Mr. Higginbotham's Catastrophe". He described it as "vividly original and dexterously managed". Other critics have favorably compared Dominicus Pike, the story's main character, to Ichabod Crane, the main character in Washington Irving's "The Legend of Sleepy Hollow". Both Pike and Crane are common men who become unlikely heroes, and each reap similar rewards for their gallantry in the end.

Nathaniel Hawthorne included this comic story in "Twice Told Tales" because he wanted the collection to appeal to a range of tastes. "Mr. Higginbotham's Catastrophe" succeeds mainly as a refreshing change of pace for devoted readers of Hawthorne. But for casual readers, it succeeds on its own. It shows the breadth of Hawthorne's talents and serves as proof he could do comedy when he chose to.

FEATHERTOP

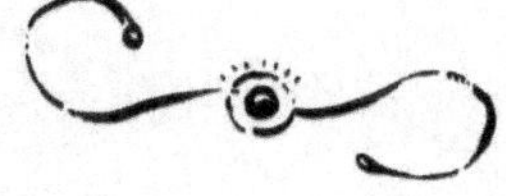

"Yo, Dickon," cried Mother Rigby, "a coal for my pipe!" The pipe was in the old dame's mouth when she said these words, but she did not stoop to light it at the hearth because no fire had been kindled there that morning. Yet as soon as the order was given, an intense red glow came out of the bowl of the pipe, followed by a whiff of smoke from Mother Rigby's lips. From where the coal came, and how it was brought forth by an invisible hand, it is impossible to know.

"Good!" said Mother Rigby, with a nod of her head. "Thank ye, Dickon! And now for making this scarecrow. Be within call, Dickon, in case I need you again."

The good woman had risen early (for as yet it was scarcely sunrise) in order to set about making a scarecrow, which she intended to put in the middle of her corn-patch. It was now the latter week of May, and the crows and blackbirds had already discovered the little, green, rolled–up leaf of the Indian corn just peeping out of the soil. She was determined, therefore, to create as lifelike a scarecrow as ever was seen, and to finish it immediately, from top to toe, so that it could begin its duty that very morning.

Now Mother Rigby was one of the most cunning and potent witches in New England. She might, with very little trouble, have made a scarecrow ugly enough to frighten a minister. But on this occasion, as she had awakened in an uncommonly pleasant humor, she resolved to produce something fine, beautiful, and splendid, rather than hideous and horrible.

"I don't want to set up a hobgoblin in my own corn-patch, and almost at my own doorstep," said Mother Rigby to herself, puffing out a whiff of smoke. "I could do it if I pleased, but I'm tired of doing marvelous things, and so I'll keep within the bounds of every-day business just for variety's sake. Besides, there is no use in scaring the little children for a mile roundabout, though it is true I am a witch."

It was settled, therefore, in her own mind, that the scarecrow should represent a fine gentleman of the period, so far as the materials at hand would allow.

The most important item of all, probably, although it made so little show, was a certain broomstick, on which Mother Rigby had taken many an airy gallop at midnight. It now served the scarecrow by way of a spinal column, or, as the unlearned phrase it, a backbone. One of its arms was a disabled scythe which used to be wielded by her late husband, Goodman Rigby, before Mother Rigby worried him out of this troublesome world. The other was composed of a spatula and a broken rung of a chair tied loosely together to make an elbow. As for its legs, the right was a hoe handle and the left an undistinguished and miscellaneous stick from the woodpile. Its lungs, stomach, and other affairs of that kind were nothing better than a meal bag stuffed with straw. Its head was admirably supplied by a somewhat withered and shriveled pumpkin, in which Mother Rigby cut two holes for the eyes and a slit for the mouth, leaving a bluish-colored knob in the middle to pass for a nose. It was really quite a respectable face.

"I've seen worse ones on human shoulders, at any rate," said Mother Rigby. "And many a fine gentleman has a pumpkin head, the same as my scarecrow."

But the clothes, in this case, would be the making of the man. So the good old woman took down from a peg an ancient plum-colored coat with relics of embroidery on its seams, cuffs, pocket-flaps, and button-holes. It was of London make, though lamentably faded and worn—patched at the elbows, tattered at the skirts, and threadbare all over. On the left breast was a round hole, where either a star of nobility had been ripped away or the hot heart of some former wearer had scorched it through and through. To match the coat there was a velvet waistcoat of very ample size. It was formerly embroidered with foliage that had been as brightly golden as the maple leaves in October, but that hue had now quite vanished out of the substance of the velvet. Next came a pair of scarlet trousers, formerly worn by a French governor. The knees had once touched the lower step of the throne of King Louis le Grand. Furthermore, Mother Rigby produced a pair of silk stockings and put them on the figure's legs, where they showed as unsubstantial as a dream, with the wooden reality of the two sticks making itself miserably apparent through the holes. Lastly, she put her dead husband's wig on the bare scalp of the pumpkin, and topped the wigged pumpkin with a dusty three-cornered hat, in which was stuck the longest tail feather of a rooster.

Then the old dame stood the figure up in a corner of her cottage and chuckled to behold its yellow semblance of a face, with its nobby little nose thrust into the air. It had a strangely self-satisfied aspect, and seemed to say, "Come look at me!"

"And you are well worth looking at, that's a fact!" said Mother Rigby, in admiration at her own handiwork. "I've made many a puppet since I've been a witch, but methinks this is the finest of them all. It's almost too good for a scarecrow. But whatever. I'll just refill my pipe and then take him out to the corn-patch."

While filling her pipe the old woman continued to gaze with almost motherly affection at the figure in the corner. To say the truth, whether it were chance, or skill, or downright witchcraft, there was something wonderfully human in this ridiculous shape, adorned with its tattered finery. And the face appeared to shrivel its yellow surface into a grin—a funny kind of expression between scorn and merriment, as if it understood itself to be a jest at mankind. The more Mother Rigby looked, the better she was pleased.

"Dickon," cried she sharply, "another coal for my pipe!"

Hardly had she spoken, than, just as before, there was a red-glowing coal atop the tobacco in the pipe. She drew in a long whiff and puffed it forth again into the bar of morning sunshine which struggled through the one dusty pane of her cottage window. Mother Rigby always liked to flavor her pipe with a coal of fire from the particular chimney corner whence this had been brought. But where that chimney corner might be, or who brought the coal from it—besides that the invisible messenger seemed to respond to the name of Dickon—who can say?

"That puppet yonder," thought Mother Rigby, still with her eyes fixed on the scarecrow, "is too good a piece of work to stand all summer in a corn-patch, frightening away the crows and blackbirds. He's capable of better things. Why, I've danced with a worse one when partners happened to be scarce at our witch meetings in the forest! What if I should let him take his chance among the other men of straw and empty fellows who go bustling about the world?"

The old witch took three or four more whiffs of her pipe and smiled.

"He'll meet plenty of his brethren at every street corner!"continued she. "Well, I didn't mean to dabble in witchcraft today any further than the lighting of my pipe. But a witch I am, and a witch I am likely to be, and there's no use trying to shirk it. I'll make a man of my scarecrow, were it only for the joke's sake!"

While muttering these words, Mother Rigby took the pipe from her own mouth and thrust it into the crevice which represented the same feature in the pumpkin face of the scarecrow.

"Puff, darling, puff!" said she. "Puff away, my fine fellow! Your life depends on it!"

This was a strange command, undoubtedly, to be addressed to a mere thing of sticks, straw, and old clothes, with nothing better than a shriveled pumpkin for a head. Nevertheless, Mother Rigby was a witch of singular power and dexterity; as soon as the old dame bade him puff, there came a whiff of smoke from the scarecrow's mouth. It was the very feeblest of whiffs, to be sure. But it was followed by another and another, each more decided than the preceding one.

"Puff away, my pet! Puff away, my pretty one!" Mother Rigby kept repeating, with her most pleasant smile. "It is the breath of life to you, and you may take my word for it."
Beyond all question the pipe was bewitched. There must have been a spell, either in the tobacco, or in the fiercely-glowing coal that so mysteriously burned on top of it, or in the pungently-aromatic smoke that rose from it. The figure, after a few doubtful attempts, at length blew forth a volley of smoke extending all the way from the obscure corner into the bar of sunshine. There it swirled and melted away among the specks of dust. It seemed an overwrought effort; for the two or three next whiffs were fainter, although the coal still glowed and threw a gleam over the scarecrow's face.

The old witch clapped her skinny hands together, and smiled encouragingly upon her handiwork. She saw that the charm worked well. The shriveled, yellow face, which up till now had been no face at all, assumed a thin, fantastic haze as if it were of human likeness.

The haze, shifting to and fro, sometimes vanished entirely, but grew more perceptible than ever with the next whiff from the pipe. The whole figure, in like manner, assumed a show of life, such as sky clouds do when, in a pastime of our own fancy, we half-deceive ourselves by imparting ill-defined shapes among them.

"Well puffed, my pretty lad!" cried old Mother Rigby. "Come, another good stout whiff, and let it be with might and main. Puff for your life, I tell you! Puff in from the very bottom of your heart, if any heart you do have or any bottom to it! Well done, again! You sucked in that mouthful as if for the pure love of it."

And then the witch beckoned to the scarecrow, throwing so much magnetic potency into her gesture that it seemed as if it must inevitably be obeyed .

"Why lurk in the corner, lazy one?" said she. "Step forth! Thou hast the world before thee!"

In obedience to Mother Rigby's word, and extending its arm as if to reach her outstretched hand, the figure made a step forward—a kind of hitch and jerk, however, rather than a step—then tottered and almost lost its balance. What could the witch expect? It was nothing, after all, but a scarecrow stuck upon two sticks.

But the strong-willed old hag scowled and beckoned. She flung the energy of her purpose so forcibly at this poor combination of rotten wood and musty straw and ragged garments, that it was compelled to show itself a man in spite of the reality of things.

It stepped into the bar of sunshine, and there it stood, poor devil of an invention that it was! It had only the thinnest wrapper of human likeness about it, far too thin to hide the stiff, rickety, discordant, faded, tattered, good-for-nothing patchwork of its substance. Standing, yes, yet ready to sink in a heap upon the floor as if conscious of its own unworthiness to be erect. The fierce old hag, showing a glimpse of her diabolic nature, began to get angry at the timid behavior of this thing which she had taken the trouble to put together.

"Puff away, wretch!" cried she, wrathfully. "Puff, puff, puff, thou thing of straw and emptiness! Thou rag or two! Thou meal bag! Thou pumpkin head! Thou nothing! Where shall I find a name vile enough to call you by? Puff, I say, and suck in thy fantastic life with the smoke, else I snatch the pipe from thy mouth and hurl you where that red coal came from!"

Thus threatened, the unhappy scarecrow could do nothing but puff away for dear life. It applied itself lustily to the pipe, and sent forth such abundant volleys of smoke that the small cottage kitchen became all vaporous. The one sunbeam struggled mistily to shine through the vapor, and could but imperfectly define the image of the cracked and dusty window pane on the opposite wall.

Mother Rigby, obscured by the vapor, loomed grimly. One arm bent, hand on hip, the other stretched towards the figure, she assumed the same pose she adopts when unleashing slow nightmares on her victims and maintains while standing bedside to enjoy their agony.

Thus, in fear and trembling the poor scarecrow did puff. But its efforts, it must be acknowledged, served an excellent purpose. For with each successive whiff, the

figure lost more and more of its dizzy and perplexing meagerness and seemed to take denser substance. Its very garments, moreover, partook of the magical change. They shone with the gloss of novelty and glistened with the skilfully embroidered gold that had long ago been rent away. And, half revealed among the smoke, a yellow face bent its lusterless eyes on Mother Rigby.

The old witch clenched her fist and shook it at the figure. She was not positively angry. She was merely acting on principle—the very highest one she could be expected to attain. It was this: feeble and apathetic natures, being incapable of better inspiration, must be stirred up by fear. But here was the crisis. What if the fear she induced were not to achieve the changes she sought to effect? Then it was her ruthless purpose to scatter the miserable sham into its original elements.

"You have a man's aspect," said she, sternly. "Now have you also the echo and mockery of a voice! I bid thee speak!"

The scarecrow gasped, struggled, and at length emitted a murmur, which was so incorporated with its smoky breath that you could scarcely tell whether it were indeed a voice or only a whiff of tobacco.

"Mother," mumbled the poor stifled voice, "be not so awful with me! I would gladly speak; but without wits, what can I say?"

"You can speak, darling! Can't you?" cried Mother Rigby, relaxing her grim expression into a smile. "And what shall you say, you ask? Say, indeed! You are of the brotherhood of the empty skull, and you demand of me what you shall say? You shall say a thousand things, and saying them a thousand times over, you shall still have said nothing! Be not afraid, I tell you! When you go into the world, wherever I send you to go, you will not lack the wherewithal to talk. Talk! Why, you shall babble like a mill-stream. You have brains enough for that, I believe!"

"At your service, mother," responded the figure.

"And that was well said, my pretty one," answered Mother Rigby. "You spoke like yourself, and meant nothing. You shall have a hundred such set phrases, and five hundred to the boot of them. And now, darling, I have taken so much pains with you and thou art so beautiful that, by my pledge, I love you better than any witch's puppet in the world. And I've made them of all sorts—clay, wax, straw, sticks, night fog, morning mist, sea foam, and chimney smoke. But thou art the very best. So give heed to what I say."

"Yes, kind mother," said the figure, "with all my heart!"

"With all thy heart!" cried the old witch, setting her hands to her sides and laughing loudly. "You have such a pretty way of speaking. With all thy heart! And you did put your hand to the left side of your waistcoat as if you really had one!"

So now, in high good humor with this fantastic creation of hers, Mother Rigby told the scarecrow that it must go and play its part in the great world, where not one man in a hundred, she affirmed, was gifted with more real substance. And that he might hold up his head with the best of them, she endowed him on the spot with an unreckonable amount of wealth. It consisted partly of a gold mine in Eldorado, ten thousand shares in a broken bubble, half a million acres of vineyard at the North Pole, a castle in the air, and a ski lodge in the Mojave desert, together with all the rents and income to be collected from these. She further made over to him the cargo of a certain ship laden with salt, which she herself, by the art of her sorcery, had caused to founder ten years before in the deepest part of mid-ocean. If the salt were not dissolved and could be brought to market, it would fetch a pretty penny among the fishermen. So that he might not lack ready money, she gave him a copper penny, being all the coin she had about her, and likewise a great deal of brass, which she applied to his forehead, thus making it yellower than ever.

"With that brass alone," said Mother Rigby, "you can pay your way all over the world. Kiss me, pretty darling! I have done my best for you."

Furthermore, that the adventurer might lack no possible advantage towards a fair start in life, this excellent old dame told him what to say to introduce himself to a certain fellow who, as magistrate, member of the council, merchant, and elder of the church, stood at the head of society in the neighboring metropolis. The introduction was neither more nor less than a single word, which Mother Rigby whispered to the scarecrow, and which the scarecrow was to whisper to the merchant.

"Gouty as the old fellow is, he'll run your errands for you once you have given him that word in his ear," said the old witch. "Mother Rigby knows the worshipful Justice Gookin, and the worshipful Justice knows Mother Rigby!"

Here the witch thrust her wrinkled face close to the puppet's, chuckling irrepressibly, and fidgeting all through her system, with delight at the idea which she meant to communicate.

"The worshipful Master Gookin," whispered she, "has a beautiful maiden as his daughter. And hear me, my pet! You have a fair outside and a pretty enough wit of your own. Yea, a pretty enough wit! You will think better of it when you have seen more of other people's wits".

"Now, with your outside and your inside, you are the very man to win a young girl's heart. Never doubt it! I tell you it shall be so. Put but a bold face on the matter, sigh, smile, flourish thy hat, thrust forth your leg like a dancing-master, put your right hand to the left side of your waistcoat, and pretty Polly Gookin is yours!"

All this while the new creature had been sucking in and exhaling the vapory fragrance of his pipe, and seemed now to continue this occupation as much for the enjoyment it afforded as because it was an essential condition of his existence. It was wonderful to see how exceedingly like a human being it behaved.

Its eyes (for it appeared to possess a pair) were bent on Mother Rigby, and at suitable junctures it nodded or shook its head. Neither did it lack words proper for the occasion: "Really! Indeed! Pray tell me! Is it possible! Upon my word! By no means! Oh! Ah! Hem!" and other such weighty utterances that imply attention, inquiry, acquiescence, or dissent on the part of the listener.

Even had you stood by and seen the scarecrow made, you could scarcely have resisted the conviction that it perfectly understood the cunning advice which the old witch poured into its counterfeit ear. The more earnestly it applied its lips to the pipe, the more distinctly was a human likeness stamped among its visible realities, the wiser grew its expression, the more life-like its gestures and movements, and the more intelligibly audible its voice.

Its garments, too, glistened so much the brighter with magical magnificence. The very pipe, in which burned the spell of all this wonderwork, ceased to appear as a smoke-blackened earthen stump. It became a finely crafted one, with painted bowl and amber mouthpiece. It might be understood, however, that as the life of this illusion seemed identical with the vapor of the pipe, the illusion would terminate exactly when the tobacco was reduced to ashes. But the witch foresaw the difficulty.

"Hold out the pipe, my precious one," said she, "while I fill it for thee again."

It was sorrowful to behold how the fine gentleman began to fade back into a scarecrow while Mother Rigby shook the ashes out of the pipe and proceeded to replenish it.

"Dickon," cried she, in her high, sharp tone, "another coal for this pipe!"

No sooner had she said it than a speck of intensely red fire was glowing within the pipe-bowl. The scarecrow, without waiting for the witch's bidding, applied the tube to his lips and drew in a few short, convulsive whiffs, which soon, however, became regular and uniform.

"Now, mine own heart's darling," said Mother Rigby, "whatever may happen to thee, you must stick to your pipe. Your life is in it. And that, at least, you know well, if you know nothing else besides. Stick to your pipe, I say! Smoke, puff, blow your cloud. And tell the people, if any question be made, that it is for your health, and that your physician orders thee to do it. And, sweet one, when you shall find your pipe getting low, go apart into some corner, fill yourself with smoke, and cry sharply, 'Dickon, a fresh pipe of tobacco!' and, 'Dickon, another coal for my pipe!' Then have it into your pretty mouth as speedily as may be. Do that, or else instead of a gallant gentleman in a gold-laced coat, you will be but a jumble of sticks and tattered clothes, and a bag of straw, and a withered pumpkin! Now depart, my treasure, and good luck go with thee!"

"Never fear, mother!" said the figure, in a stout voice, and sending forth a courageous whiff of smoke, "I will thrive, if an honest man and a gentleman may!"

"Oh, you will be the death of me!" cried the old witch, convulsed with laughter. "That was well said. If an honest man and a gentleman may! You play your part to perfection. Get along now and be like a smart fellow; and, as a man of pith and substance with a brain and what they call a heart, and all else that a man should have, I will wager on your head against any other thing on two legs. I hold myself a better witch than yesterday because of you. Did not I make you? And I defy any witch in New England to make such another! Here—take my staff along with you!"

The staff, though it was but a plain oaken stick, immediately took the aspect of a gold-headed cane.

"That gold head has as much sense in it as your own," said Mother Rigby, "and it will guide you straight to worshipful Master Gookin's door. Get gone, my pretty pet, my darling, my precious one, my treasure. And if anyone asks your name, it is Feathertop. For you have a feather in your hat, and I thrust a handful of feathers into the hollow of your head. And your wig, too, is of the fashion they call Feathertop. So be it then—Feathertop is thy name!"

And, issuing from the cottage, Feathertop strode manfully towards town. Mother Rigby stood at the threshold, well pleased to see how the sunbeams glistened on him, as if all his magnificence were real, and how diligently and lovingly he smoked his pipe, and how handsomely he walked in spite of a little stiffness of his legs. She watched him go, then threw a witch benediction after her darling when a turn of the road snatched him from her view.

Later that same morning, when the principal street of the neighboring town was just at its peak of life and bustle, a stranger of very distinguished figure was seen on the sidewalk. His carriage and garments suggested nothing short of nobility. He managed a gold-headed cane with airy grace, peculiar to the fine gentlemen of the period. He wore a richly-embroidered, plum-colored coat with a glistening star upon its breast. He wore a waistcoat of costly velvet magnificently adorned with golden foliage, a pair of splendid scarlet trousers, and the finest and glossiest of white silk stockings. His head was covered with a wig, so daintily powdered and adjusted, that it would have been sacrilege to disorder it with a hat. Thus, he carried his gold-laced and snowy feathered hat beneath his arm. And, to give the highest possible finish to his equipment, he wore lace ruffles at his wrist. They bore a most airy delicacy, which sufficiently showed how idle and aristocratic must be the hands they half concealed.

It was a remarkable point in the appearance of this brilliant individual that he held in his left hand a fantastic kind of a pipe, with an exquisitely painted bowl and an amber mouthpiece. This he applied to his lips as often as every five or six paces, and inhaled a deep whiff of smoke, which, after being retained a moment in his lungs, might be seen to seep gracefully from his mouth and nostrils. As may well be supposed, the street was all astir to find out the stranger's name.

"It is some great nobleman, beyond question," said one of the townspeople. "Do you see the star at his breast?"

"Nay; it is too bright to be seen," said another. "Yes; he must has to be a nobleman, as you say. But by what means, do you think, can his lordship have voyaged or traveled to this place? There has been no vessel from the old country for a month past. And if he have arrived overland from the southward, pray where are his attendants and horse-drawn carriage?"

"He needs no carriage to set off his rank," remarked a third.

"If he came among us in rags, nobility would shine through a hole in the elbow of his coat. I never saw such dignity of aspect. He has old Norman blood in his veins, I would bet."

"I rather take him to be a Dutchman, or one of your high Germans," said another citizen. "The men of those countries have always a pipe at their mouths."

"And so has a Turk," answered his companion. "But, in my judgment, this stranger has been bred at the French court. It is there he learned politeness and grace of manner, which none understand so well as the nobility of France. That walking gait, now! A vulgar spectator might deem it stiff—

he might call it a hitch and jerk—but, to my eye, it has an unspeakable majesty, and must have been acquired by constant observation of the graceful carriage of the Grand Monarch."

"More probably a Spaniard," said another, "and hence his yellow complexion; or, most likely, he is from Havana, or from some port on the Spanish main."

"Yellow or not," cried a lady, "he is a beautiful man!—so tall, so slender! Such a fine, noble face, with so well-shaped a nose, and all that delicacy of expression about the mouth! And, bless me, how bright his star is! It positively shoots out flames!"

"So do your eyes, fair lady," said the stranger, with a bow and a flourish of his pipe; for he was just passing at the instant. "Upon my honor, they have quite dazzled me."

"Was there ever so original and exquisite a compliment?" murmured the lady, in an ecstasy of delight.

Amid the general admiration excited by the stranger's appearance, there were only two dissenting voices. One was that of an impertinent mongrel dog, which, after sniffing at the heels of the glistening figure, put its tail between its legs and skulked into its master's back yard, emitting a screechy howl. The other dissenter was a young child who squalled at the fullest stretch of his lungs and babbled some unintelligible nonsense about a pumpkin.

Feathertop meanwhile pursued his way along the street. Except for the few complimentary words to the lady, and now and then a slight inclination of the head to reward the profound reverences of the bystanders, he seemed wholly absorbed in his pipe.

There needed no other proof of his rank and consequence than the perfect composure with which he carried himself, while the curiosity and admiration of the town swelled almost into clamor around him. With a crowd gathering behind his footsteps, he finally reached the mansion-house of the worshipful Justice Gookin, entered the gate, ascended the steps to the front door, and knocked. In the interim, before his summons was answered, the stranger was observed to shake the ashes out of his pipe.

"What did he say in that sharp voice?" inquired one of the spectators.

"Nay, I know not," answered his friend. "But the sun dazzles my eyes strangely. How dim and faded his lordship looks all of a sudden! Bless my wits, what is the matter with me?"

"The wonder is," said the other, "that his pipe, which was out only an instant ago, should be all alight again, and with the reddest coal I ever saw. There is something mysterious about this stranger. What a whiff of smoke was that! Dim and faded did you call him? Why, as he turns about the star on his breast is all ablaze."

"It is, indeed," said his companion; "and it will go near to dazzle pretty Polly Gookin, whom I see peeping at it out of the chamber window."

The door being now opened, Feathertop turned to the crowd. There was a mysterious kind of a smile, if it might not better be called a grin or grimace, upon his face. But of all the throng that beheld him, not an individual appears to have possessed insight enough to decisively detect the illusive character of the stranger except the squalling little child and the howling mongrel dog. He made a stately bend of his body like a great man acknowledging the reverence of the meaner sort, and vanished into the house to meet the merchant and go in quest of the pretty Polly Gookin.

Polly was a damsel of a soft, round figure, with light hair and blue eyes, and a fair, rosy face, which seemed neither very shrewd nor very simple. This young lady had caught a glimpse of the glistening stranger while standing on the threshold, and had immediately put on a laced cap, a string of beads, her finest kerchief, and her stiffest deep-pink petticoat in preparation for the interview. Hurrying from her chamber to the parlor, she had ever since been viewing herself in the large looking-glass and practicing pretty airs—now a smile, now a ceremonious dignity of aspect, and now a softer smile than the former, kissing her hand likewise, tossing her head, and managing her fan; while within the mirror an unsubstantial little maid repeated every gesture and did all the foolish things that Polly did, but without making her ashamed of them.

In short, it was the fault of pretty Polly's ability, not her will, if she failed to be as complete an imitation as the illustrious Feathertop himself. Having thus tampered with her own simplicity, the witch's phantom might well hope to win her.

No sooner did Polly hear her father's gouty footsteps approaching the parlor door, accompanied with the stiff clatter of Feathertop's high-heeled shoes, than she seated herself bolt upright and innocently began warbling a song. "Polly! daughter Polly!" cried the old merchant. "Come hither, child."

Master Gookin's aspect, as he opened the door, was doubtful and troubled.

"This gentleman," continued he, presenting the stranger, "is the Chevalier Feathertop—nay, I beg his pardon, my Lord Feathertop—who hath brought me a token of remembrance from an ancient friend of mine. Pay your duty to his lordship, child, and honor him as his quality deserves."

After these few words of introduction, the worshipful magistrate immediately left the room. But, even in that brief moment, had the fair Polly glanced aside at her father instead of devoting herself wholly to the brilliant guest,

she might have taken warning of some mischief near at hand. For the old man was nervous, fidgety, and very pale. Attempting a smile of courtesy, he had deformed his face with a hyper-exaggerated grin. When Feathertop's back was turned, he exchanged the grin for a scowl and shook his fist and stamped his gouty foot—an incivility which brought instant and painful retribution along with it.

The truth appears to have been that Mother Rigby's word of introduction, whatever it might be, had operated far more on the rich merchant's fears than on his good will. Moreover, being a man of wonderfully acute observation, he had noticed that the painted figures on the bowl of Feathertop's pipe were in motion. Looking more closely he became convinced that these figures were a party of little demons, each with horns and a tail. They danced hand in hand, with gestures of diabolical merriment, round the circumference of the pipe bowl.

And as if to confirm his suspicions, the star on Feathertop's breast sparked actual flames and threw a flickering gleam upon the walls, ceiling, and floor of a dusky passageway as Master Gookin ushered his guest through to the parlor.

With such sinister signs appearing, it is not surprising the merchant should have felt that he was committing his daughter to a very questionable acquaintance.

In his secret soul, he cursed the artfully infused elegance of Feathertop's manners. He watched this brilliant individual bow, smile, and put his hand on his heart. He watched him inhale a long, luxurious whiff from his pipe and then, with an exhale, enrich the atmosphere with a visible sigh of smoky, fragrant vapor.

Gladly would poor Master Gookin have thrust his dangerous guest into the street. But there was a constraint and terror within him. Could this respectable old merchant have given a pledge to the evil one at an earlier period of his life, and was he now redeeming it by the sacrifice of his daughter?

It so happened that the parlor door was partly of glass, shaded by a silken curtain, the folds of which hung a little awry. So strong was the merchant's interest in witnessing what was to ensue between the fair Polly and the gallant Feathertop that, after leaving the room, he could not refrain from peeping through the crevice of the curtain.

However, besides the trifles previously noticed, he saw nothing very miraculous that would confirm his idea that a supernatural peril threatened the pretty Polly. Was he needlessly concerned? The stranger, it is true, was evidently a thorough and practiced man of the world. But was he merely the sort of person a parent ought not trust with a simple, young girl without due watchfulness for the result.

The worthy magistrate, who had been familiar with all degrees and qualities of mankind, kept his eyes glued on the pair. He could not help but notice that every motion and gesture of the distinguished visitor came in its proper place; nothing had been left rude or native in him. Perhaps it was this conventionalism that made Feathertop seem a work of art. And yet, because he hardly had substance enough to cast a shadow on the floor, there was also a type of ghastliness and awe about him. Feathertop made a wild, extravagant, and fantastical impression indeed, as if his life and being were akin to the smoke that curled upward from his pipe.

Pretty Polly Gookin noticed none of this. The pair were now promenading the room: Feathertop with his dainty stride and no less dainty grimace, the girl with a native maidenly grace, just touched, not spoiled, by a slightly affected manner, which she seemed to have caught

from the perfect artifice of her companion. The longer
the interview continued, the more charmed was pretty
Polly, until, within the first quarter of an hour (as the old
magistrate noted by his watch), she had evidently begun
to fall in love. Was it witchcraft that subdued her in such a
hurry, or was the poor child's heart so fervent that it melted
her with its own warmth? No matter what Feathertop
said, his words found depth and reverberation in her ear;
no matter what he did, his action was heroic to her eye. By
this time there was a blush on Polly's cheek, a tender smile
about her mouth, and a liquid softness in her glance.

Meanwhile, the star kept glittering on Feathertop's breast,
and the little demons raced about the circumference of his
pipe bowl with more frantic merriment than ever. O pretty
Polly Gookin, why should these imps rejoice so madly that
a silly maiden's heart was about to be given to a shadow?
Is it such an unusual misfortune, so rare a triumph to cause
such celebration?

By and by Feathertop paused, and throwing himself into
an imposing attitude, seemed to summon the fair girl to
survey his figure and resist him longer if she could. His
star, his embroidery, his buckles glowed at that instant with
unutterable splendor. The picturesque hues of his attire took
a richer depth of coloring. There was a gleam and polish
over his whole presence telling of the perfect witchery of
well-ordered manners.

The maiden raised her eyes and suffered them to linger upon her companion with a bashful and admiring gaze. Then, as if she desired to judge of what value her own simple beauty might have side by side with so much brilliancy, she cast a glance towards the full-length looking-glass in front of which they happened to be standing. It was one of the truest plates of looking-glass in the world and incapable of flattery. No sooner did the images reflected therein meet Polly's eye than she shrieked, shrank from the stranger's side, gazed at him for a moment in the wildest dismay, and sank insensible upon the floor.

Feathertop likewise looked towards the mirror and there beheld, not the glittering mockery of his outside show, but a picture of the sordid patchwork of his real composition stripped of all witchcraft. The wretched sham! We almost pity him. He threw up his arms with an expression of despair that far exceeded any hope he had ever displayed to be reckoned human. Perchance this was the only time since the so-often-empty and deceptive life of mortals began its course after Eden that an illusion had seen and fully recognized itself.

Mother Rigby was seated by her kitchen hearth in the twilight of this eventful day, and had just shaken the ashes out of a new pipe, when she heard a hurried tramp along the road. Yet it did not seem so much the tramp of human footsteps as the clatter of sticks or the rattling of dry bones. "Ha!" thought the old witch, "what step is that? Whose skeleton is out of its grave now, I wonder?"

A figure burst headlong into the cottage door. It was Feathertop! His pipe was still alight; the star still flamed upon his breast; the embroidery still glowed upon his garments; nor had he lost, in any degree or manner that could be estimated, the look that made him one with our mortal brotherhood.

But yet, in some indescribable way (as is the case with all that has deluded us when once found out), the poor reality was apparent beneath the cunning deception.

"What has gone wrong?" demanded the witch. "Did that sniffling hypocrite thrust my darling from his door? The villain! I'll set twenty fiends to torment him till he offers you his daughter on his bended knees!"

"No, mother," said Feathertop despondently; "it was not that."

"Did the girl scorn my precious one?" asked Mother Rigby, her fierce eyes glowing like two coals of hell. "I'll cover her face with pimples! Her nose shall be as red as the coal in thy pipe! Her front teeth shall drop out! In a week from now she shall not be worth having!"

"Let her alone, mother," answered poor Feathertop; "the girl was half won; and methinks a kiss from her sweet lips might have made me altogether human."

But he added, after a brief pause and then a howl of self-contempt, "I've seen myself, mother! I've seen myself for the wretched, ragged, empty thing I am! I will exist no longer!"

Snatching the pipe from his mouth, he flung it with all his might against the chimney, and at the same instant sank upon the floor, a medley of straw and tattered garments, with some sticks protruding from the heap, and a shriveled pumpkin in the midst. The eye-holes were now dull. But the rudely-carved gap, that just before had been a mouth, still seemed to twist itself into a despairing grin, and was so far human.

"Poor fellow!" said Mother Rigby, with a rueful glance at the relics of her ill-fated creation. "My poor, dear, pretty Feathertop! There are thousands upon thousands of clowns and charlatans in the world, made up of just such a jumble of worn-out, forgotten, and good-for-nothing trash as you were! Yet they live in fair repute, and never see themselves for what they are. Why should my poor puppet be the only one to know himself and perish for it?"

While thus muttering, the witch had filled a fresh pipe and held the stem between her fingers, as doubtful whether to thrust it into her own mouth or Feathertop's.

"Poor Feathertop!" she continued. "I could easily give him another chance and send him forth again tomorrow. But no—his feelings are too tender, his sensibilities too deep. He seems to have too much heart to bustle for his own advantage in such an empty and heartless world. Well! Well! I'll make a scarecrow of him after all. 'Tis an innocent and useful vocation, and will suit my darling well. If each of his human brethren had as fit a one, it would be the better for mankind. As for this pipe, I need it more than he."

So saying, Mother Rigby put the stem between her lips. "Dickon!" cried she, in her high, sharp tone, "another coal for my pipe!"

the end

FEATHERTOP

Feathertop was the last story Hawthorne wrote. Most literary critics do not rank it with his best. They usually find the story too far-fetched and its moral message too obvious. Both these criticisms may be valid, but it's also very difficult to please literary critics. Did they overlook Feathertop's high entertainment value? Mother Rigby certainly makes her disdain for human phoniness very obvious, but she does so with humorous digs and disses that have held up very well over time.

And when Feathertop gained self-awareness, when he realized he was but a scarecrow stuffed with straw, his surrender to truth contrasted sharply with the humans he met who were blindly or casually superficial. At least one critic thinks that's a very nice satiric poke at society. So maybe Hawthorne should get credit for blending effective satire with a far-fetched plot to create a highly entertaining story.

Finally, on a basic emotional level, who doesn't feel at least a little sympathy for Feathertop? He did not choose the task he was sent off to accomplish—without success—and he did not seek personal glorification—fleeting as it was. He meets a sorry end, and what was his fatal flaw? He was endowed with too much good-heartedness to survive in the world. How sad!

NATHANIEL HAWTHORNE
(1804-1864)

Nathaniel Hawthorne was born on July 4, 1804 in Salem, Massachusetts, a city where he spent much of his life and set many of his literary works. Drawn to writing at an early age (in his youth he published a newspaper, The Spectator), Hawthorne published over 100 short stories, sketches, novels, children's stories, and non-fiction pieces during his career.

Nathaniel Hawthorne is widely recognized as one of America's greatest authors. He had a special talent for pin-pointing and describing the deep-seated motivations of his characters. He also accurately assessed the American character and experience of his own and preceding generations. As it so happens, his assessment also applies to present-day American society.

But besides all that, and maybe above all, Mr. Hawthorne told entertaining tales with great dexterity. His prose was stylish, often almost poetic. He had a fanciful imagination and a deep moral sensibility. There have been few writers in any age who could render scenes more visually or expose the moral fiber of characters more ably than Nathaniel Hawthorne. His fame will surely endure.

Marc Johnson-Pencook is an illustrator, animator, and muralist. He lives in Minneapolis, Minnesota. His illustrations appear in books, periodicals, gallery shows and private collections, and his murals adorn many walls and ceilings in public places and private spaces in the Twin Cities and beyond. In addition, Marc composes and performs rock music—he currently plays drums for "Ozmo Stone"—a rock band based in Minneapolis. Marc can be contacted at: www.illustratormarc.com

Jerome Tiller lives in Minneapolis, Minnesota. He is co-owner of ArtWrite Productions, a publishing company bent on making education and reading more pleasurable for youth. Adapted Classics, an imprint of ArtWrite Productions, uses fine-art illustrations to introduce classic stories to young readers. Learn more about Jerome, his co-owner son Paul, and their company at: artwriteproductions.com and adaptedclassics.com